This book belongs to

Erika Driscoll

Published by Advance Publishers

© 1998 Disney Enterprises, Inc.

All rights reserved. Printed in the United States.
No part of this book may be reproduced or copied in any form
without the written permission of the copyright owner.

Written by Ronald Kidd
Illustrated by Kevin Kidney and Jody Daily
Produced by Bumpy Slide Books

ISBN: 1-57973-011-6

10 9 8 7 6 5 4 3 2 1

Walt Disney's

Lady and the TRAMP

A Trusty Old Pal

Lady and the Tramp's puppies were very excited. Their mother and father were taking them out for a special treat.

"Where are we going, Mama?" asked Fluffy.

"You'll see, dear," said Lady. "It's a surprise."

Scamp, who was always in a hurry, raced in circles around his father, saying, "Are we there yet? Are we there yet?"

"Pretty soon," Tramp answered, smiling.

"But when?" asked Scamp.

They rounded a corner and Tramp said, "Now!"

Up ahead was Tony's Italian restaurant. "Welcome, my four-footed friends," said Tony, as he brought out a plate of spaghetti and meatballs. When the pups were finished, Tony said, "And a-now, time for my beautiful cake! Let me see, where did I put it?"

Tony found the cake a moment later, but someone was already digging in. Looking at Scamp covered in frosting, Tony couldn't help but laugh. The rest of the dogs joined in the fun, and soon all of them were sharing the delicious dessert.

When the puppies arrived home, they found another surprise waiting for them. It was Trusty and Jock, the two dogs who lived on their block.

Jock, a Scottie, told Tramp the reason for their visit. "You see, lad, me owners and Trusty's owners are taking a wee trip together. They want me to go along, but Trusty here is a bit old to travel. Could he stay with you for a week? That is, if it's no trouble."

"Trouble?" said Tramp. "Don't be silly. Trusty saved my life!"

The puppies gathered around the old bloodhound. "Really?" they asked. "Is that true, Uncle Trusty?"

"Well," said Trusty, "as my grandpappy, Old Reliable, used to say . . . I don't recollect if I ever told you about Old Reliable, did I?"

As Trusty launched into a story, Lady gazed fondly at him. "Don't worry, Jock," she said. "We'll be happy to have Trusty stay with us."

For the first few days, the puppies found it exciting to have their Uncle Trusty around. They tumbled over his back. They played hide-and-seek behind him. They listened intently to his stories of the good old days, when he and Old Reliable used to track criminals for the police force.

It wasn't long, though, before the puppies began to notice some things that weren't so exciting about their new houseguest. Trusty always got to eat first, and when he did, he ate very, very slowly.

He took long afternoon naps on the stairs, where the puppies were always tripping over him. When he slept, he snored, and his snoring was as loud as a foghorn.

Worst of all, his stories grew longer by the day,
until the puppies could barely wait until he finished.
Scamp, always the impatient one, found it harder
and harder to listen.

One day, Trusty had just begun a story in the usual way: "Now, as my grandpappy, Old Reliable, used to say . . . I don't recollect if I ever told you about Old Reliable, did I?"

Finally Scamp had had enough. "Yes!" he exclaimed. "You already told us about Old Reliable — about a thousand times!"

Trusty looked up at him, confused. "I did?"

"Of course you did," said Scamp, "over and over and over again! It's boring!"

The other puppies' eyes grew wide. They looked uncomfortably at each other, then wandered off. Scamp looked at Trusty's hurt face and backed away. "I think I hear Mother calling," he said.

The next morning, the puppies came bounding
down the stairs for breakfast. As they did, they
noticed something different. There was no dog to
trip over, and no loud snoring to greet them.
Trusty was gone.

They looked all around the house — under the stairs, in the kitchen, and in the playroom. Then they went outside and searched the yard. But there was no sign of Trusty anywhere.

The puppies went to their parents and told them Trusty had left.

"Why would he do that?" asked Tramp.

No one answered, until Scamp said, "I think I know." He repeated what he had said to Trusty the day before.

"Scamp!" said Lady. "You must have hurt his feelings."

Scamp hung his head. "I didn't mean to. I'm sorry."

"We've got to find him," said Tramp. "Scamp and I will nose around the old neighborhood to see what we can find. Pidge, you take the others and check the dog pound."

Fluffy, Ruffy, and Scooter followed Lady out of the yard, calling as they went, "Trusty! Trusty, where are you?"

They hurried along the sidewalk until houses gave way to stores, and stores to factories. Then, in the distance, they saw a sign: City Dog Pound.

"Stay out of sight," Lady told the puppies. "I'll be right back."

She sneaked inside the pound and tiptoed along the rows of cages. There were beagles, Afghans, greyhounds, boxers, poodles, and Chihuahuas. But there were no bloodhounds.

"Hey, what are you doing? Did you get out of your cage?" a man called out.

Lady turned and saw the dogcatcher standing in the doorway. She gathered her courage and bolted straight past him out the door.

"Follow me," she told the puppies when she reached them. "We're going home!"

In another part of town, Tramp had taken Scamp
to look around the old neighborhood, hoping to find
Trusty. Sure enough, a dog named Peg had seen him
that very morning. "He seemed to be headed for the
woods," Peg told them.

"Thanks, Peg," said Tramp. "You're a pal. We'll go look there."

"Oh, one more thing," Peg added. "There's a rough character who's been hanging around those woods — a big, mean stray. Be careful!"

Soon Scamp and his father entered the woods and began sniffing for Trusty's familiar scent. Suddenly a screech filled the air. Scamp jumped, his heart pounding, as he watched a dark shape settle onto a tree branch.

"Don't worry, son," said Tramp. "It's just an owl."

Scamp gazed up into the tree. "Mr. Owl," he said, "have you seen our friend, Trusty?"

"Who?" asked the owl.

"Trusty," Scamp said. "He's a bloodhound."

"Who?" asked the owl.

Scamp sighed. "Never mind."

As they moved off down the path once more, there was a loud crash.

"Follow me!" called Tramp as they raced in the direction of the noise. Soon they found a beaver standing proudly next to a fallen tree.

"Hello," said Tramp. "Don't you think you should warn folks *before* the tree falls?"

The beaver grinned sheepishly. "Funny, that's what the last guy said."

"The last guy?" asked Tramp.

"Some old bloodhound. He headed off that way," the beaver said, pointing.

Scamp raced along behind his father, struggling to keep up. As they hurried through the woods, Scamp noticed something out of the corner of his eye. It was big and brown, like Trusty. Scamp knew he should call out to his father, but he kept silent.

He felt bad about hurting the old bloodhound's feelings and was eager to make up for it. If Scamp could be the one to find Trusty, surely everyone would forgive him. Maybe he'd even be a hero!

Turning away from the path, Scamp began moving slowly toward the trees.

"Hello," he said softly. "Hello?"

"Hello, my friend," growled a deep voice. Then out of the bushes came the largest dog Scamp had ever seen.

"I-I was looking for someone else," said
Scamp as he turned to leave. But one of the
dog's giant paws blocked his way. The dog's
massive head sank lower and lower, teeth
flashing, jaws opening wide.

All at once a familiar voice drawled, "Ah believe Ah'd let the pup pass if Ah were you."

The dog stopped growling. Frowning, he looked up and saw Trusty step out from behind a tree. Then, as Scamp watched, an amazing thing happened.

The dog's ears flattened against his head. "I guess I'll be going now," he said in a soft, meek voice. Then he slunk off into the woods.

Scamp stared at Trusty, but the old bloodhound just shrugged. "That rascal and I had a few run-ins when I was with the police. After that, we got along just fine."

A few days later the neighbors returned, and Jock came over to visit.

"Did you enjoy your vacation?" Lady asked.

"Ay, lass," replied the Scottie, "it was a grand trip. The only bad part was that I missed me good friend Trusty. So, what d'ye think? Is he ready to go home?"

"Well," she answered, "I'm afraid there's a slight problem."

Jock's eyes narrowed with concern. "Speak up then, what is it?"

"You see," said Tramp, "while you were gone, Trusty ran away."

Just then, the old bloodhound lumbered around the corner, surrounded by Lady and Tramp's puppies. Tramp continued, "And ever since he came home, the pups won't let him out of their sight!"

As Jock watched, Scamp raced around in circles, begging, "Please, Uncle Trusty, just tell us one more story."

Trusty looked down at Scamp and smiled. Then, gathering the puppies around him, he settled beneath a shade tree.

"Well," he began, "as my grandpappy, Old Reliable, used to say . . . I don't recollect if I ever told you about Old Reliable, did I?"

When Scamp yearns for adventure,
He just listens to old Trusty,
Whose stories are exciting,
Though his memory might be rusty!
All older folks have tales to tell
And each time that they do,
Enjoy your time together
While you're learning something new.